IMOGENE'S ANTLERS

IMOGENE'S ANTLERS
By David Small

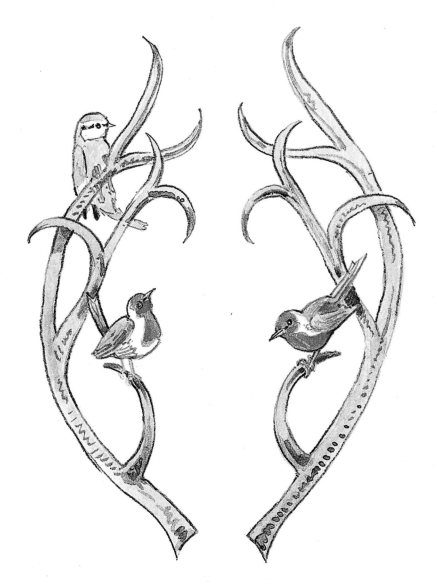

CROWN PUBLISHERS ♕ NEW YORK

Published by Crown Publishers, a division of Random House, Inc., 1540 Broadway, New York, NY 10036. Originally published by Crown Publishers, a division of Random House, Inc., in 1985.

www.randomhouse.com/kids

Library of Congress Cataloging-in-Publication Data
Small, David, 1945–
Imogene's antlers.
Summary: One Thursday Imogene wakes up with a pair of antlers growing out of her head and causes a sensation wherever she goes.
1. Children's stories, American. [1. Humorous stories]
I. Title.
PZ7.S638Im   1985   [E]   84-12085

ISBN   0-375-81048-X (trade)
           0-375-91048-4 (lib. bdg.)

Printed in Hong Kong
September 2000

10   9   8   7   6   5   4   3   2   1

This edition first published in 2000.
CROWN and colophon are trademarks of Random House, Inc.

To A.B., L.D. and little O.

— D.S.

On Thursday, when Imogene
woke up, she found she
had grown antlers.

Getting dressed was difficult,

and going through a door
now took some thinking.

Imogene started down
for breakfast...

but got
hung up.

"OH!!"
Imogene's mother
fainted away.

The doctor poked, and prodded, and scratched his chin.

He could find nothing wrong.

The school principal glared at Imogene but had no advice to offer.

Her brother, Norman, consulted
the encyclopedia, and then announced
that Imogene had turned into a rare
form of miniature elk!

Imogene's mother fainted again
and was carried upstairs to bed.

Imogene went into the kitchen.
Lucy, the kitchen maid, had her
sit by the oven to dry some towels.
"Lovely antlers," said Lucy.

The cook, Mrs. Perkins, gave
Imogene a doughnut, then
decked her out with several more
and sent her into the garden
to feed the birds.

"You'll be lots of fun
to decorate,
come Christmas!"
said Mrs. Perkins.

Later, Imogene wandered upstairs.
She found the whole family
in Mother's bedroom.

"Doughnuts anyone?" she asked.

Her mother said, "Imogene, we have decided there is only one thing to do. We must hide your antlers under a hat!"

Norman telephoned the milliner.

EMERGENCY HAT SERVICE

"We Hide your Head in a HURRY!"

Call 637-9849

At three o'clock
the milliner
arrived.

Rapidly
he sketched
a few designs,

then set to work.

"Voilà!" said the milliner.

"Bravo! Bravissimo!" cried his assistants.

THUD! Imogene's mother had to be carried away once more.

After dinner,
Imogene practiced
her piano
lesson.

Then, yawning,
she folded her music...

kissed the family...

and went to bed.

Imogene sighed,
remembering the long,
eventful day.

On Friday, when Imogene
woke up, the antlers had disappeared.

When she came down to
breakfast, the family was overjoyed
to see her back to normal...

until she came into the room.